The Town Called *Sacrifice*

WRITTEN BY

SANDRA THURMAN

ILLUSTRATED BY

LILYAN WEST

DESIGNED BY

CHAE LU HINSON

Print information available on the last page

Rev. date: 08/30/2019

To order additional copies of this book, contact:
Xlibris
1-888-795-4274
www.Xlibris.com
Orders@Xlibris.com

Dedication

❖❖❖❖❖

Dedicated to small town families who provided sons and daughters to serve, fight, and sometimes die so that we can continue to enjoy our freedom

Following her multicultural historical fiction work, *Georgia's Chilly Winds and Warm Breezes*, Sandra Thurman penned a patriotic journey of discovery entitled *The Town Called Sacrifice.*

Believing that young people should respect the past, live in the present, and prepare for the future, she felt this book met a need. Living with her husband, her dog, and three cats, Thurman enjoys reading, writing, and sports. She considers every day a blessing from God and enjoys each one.

Happy reading!

Pride, patriotism, family, and a small town: what do these have in common? The town called Sacrifice, of course!

Believing that it is important to live in the present, look forward to the future, and glean from the past, Sadie investigates her parents' new architectural venture.

Making friends with a local about her age, Sadie dives into the town's history and invites her new friend Si to join her.

A journey of discovery unlocks secrets of her family's story.

Sadie and Si learn the importance of family and what it means to know and to understand one's past. They grow to appreciate the patriotism of a small town.

It was the last day in that terrible history class! I mean who needs to know what happened way back then when there are so many exciting things occurring now? After completing my test, I sat dreamily envisioning my summer—sleeping late, swimming, camps, beach trips, mountain stays, and, of course, vacation! The obnoxious sound of the final bell returned me to the present.

Racing down the hall, out the front door, and down what seemed like hundreds of steps, I reached Mom's waiting car. And then I saw it, that expression on her face, the one that said we were leaving normalcy and traveling into the dark crevices of the past.

"Oh, you'll just love it! The house is straight from the old South, with two stories, hardwood floors, shutters, a wrap around veranda, and a winding staircase." On and on she chattered just like a happy magpie.

My parents had no concept of my perfect summer: waking up when I got ready, going to sleep when my favorite show was over, taking trips to the beach, sunning and swimming to my heart's content, reading and exercising at my own pace, talking to and visiting with my friends, and, of course, spending time with my spoiled all-American mutt who always seemed to think she was neglected.

But no, here I was in the back seat of my mom's packed-to-the-brim SUV with Dad following closely in his work van.

After an hour or so, Mom turned left onto a bumpy cobblestone driveway, and we rattled along the narrow lane. Huge oaks with low hanging Spanish moss, looking rather like a bridal train in a storybook wedding, lined the drive.

But that's where the fairy tale ended. What had once been a house loomed like an over-sized elephant, with shutters hanging off the hinges, a wrap-around porch appearing more like a railroad track due to missing planks, and a beautiful winding staircase I could see through the door looking as if Sherman had marched over it with all of his troops.

To my parents, it was a true southern farmhouse straight from the mid 1800's. My mom saw chivalry and etiquette, southern barbeques, and large lawn parties—hoop skirts, floppy hats, and corsets with so many stays and laces that the one who wore it couldn't get a breath.

As my dad looked at the house, his eyes grew green with the successful agriculture he imagined. His nose twitched as he smelled the fresh earth. His ears perked up as he heard birds singing, dogs barking, and horses galloping down the lane.

Running their business from a distance had become the norm for the past few summers, but I must admit, escaping the stresses of the everyday work world was calming.

"Just leave everything in the car," Mom said. "Let's look things over first."

I grabbed my bike from the rack on her vehicle and answered, "I think I'll scout out the town first!"

The Town

It was like most of the small towns my parents had introduced me to over the years. One main street contained a drug store, a barber shop with a twirling candy striped pole, and a hardware store where men sat around the wood stove, summer or winter, catching up on news, drinking coffee and eating some sinfully delicious buns one of their wives had made.

I noticed a small cafe, parked my bike in the stand, and entered. A jingling bell announced my presence. Everyone turned to look at the scrawny kid with a ponytail who did not quite belong. As a waitress approached, I could almost feel the quizzical stares of other customers. The lemonade I had wanted lost its appeal. Instead of ordering, I asked for directions to the First Baptist Church, a safe question and destination, I thought.

The Drugstore

I exited the cafe, mounted my bike, and started pedaling down the street. Out of the corner of my eye, I noticed a red headed boy sweeping the sidewalk in front of the drugstore. As I got closer, he looked up, flashed a quick grin, and said, "Hello! I'm Si, short for Silas. What's your name?"

"I'm Sadie," I answered.

With a couple of swipes of his broom, he finished his job and called, "It's really hot out here! Let's go in. My dad's the pharmacist, and I'm the resident soda jerk and dishwasher. How about you?"

"Well, my folks just purchased the old McCay house on the outskirts of town. They buy abandoned mansions and fix them up to sell. While they lose themselves in the house, I find myself in the community."

We entered the glass door, and I plopped into the nearest booth, while Si fixed us both some lemonade.

Sipping my drink, I observed the old fashioned drugstore. An antique soda fountain with its polished marble top and circular red stools impressed me. A few tables, chairs and booths of the same color scheme surrounded us. One could tell they had stood the test of time.

Having inherited some of my parents' imagination, I could see young people dancing on the worn black and white checkered linoleum floor. I could hear music from the old juke box and laughter and conversation between "first loves." I could see the sad smiles through proud tears as boys one-by-one shared their upcoming military deployments. After all, they were young American men who felt the pride of country. Nothing else would do for them but to join the military.

The pharmacy in the back was almost an afterthought to the timeless setting in the store's front.

Si's voice rang down aisle two, bringing me back to the present. "Hey, Sadie, my dad closes at 5:00. We could go riding and I could show you some of the local sights."

"Sounds good to me. I'll just need to let my parents know. Meet you here at five." And with that, I left.

As I pedaled back toward my new address for the next few months, I noticed that the old hardware store, grocery and general store looked like they had come straight from a history book. Excited about my discoveries, I arrived home seemingly in a flash.

"Hello, where have you been?" my parents asked in unison.

"Oh, I just rode into town to see what it was like and made a friend named Si. His dad owns the pharmacy. If it's okay with you guys, we're going to ride our bikes, and he's going to show me around the town."

"It should be fine," Dad said. "I met Seth Bartlett on my initial visit. He seemed like a nice man."

"Why don't you invite Si to have dinner with us?" Mom asked.

My parents instructed me to be back by 6:30 to go eat at a cafe they'd seen just off the interstate.

The Ride

Following an extensive tour of the small town, Si said, "Let's go this way." He pedaled casually toward East Main Street. While riding, we talked of school subjects, hobbies, and the weather. Turning left onto Magnolia Lane, Si pointed out different farms and landmarks. "Sherman and his troops camped here one time," he noted. "And General Robert E. Lee stopped at this once regal home to discuss farming business. Cotton and tobacco filled these fields. Now they lie bare mostly due to the town's economy."

All of a sudden, my eyes widened, my mouth flew open, and I asked, "What's that?"

Si stopped his bicycle and got off in front of a sign which read "Private Property: Keep Out!"

"It's the old Reynolds house," he answered and continued speaking with a puzzled look. "Legend has it that it is exactly the same as it was when Mr. Reynolds passed away. The rumor mill in town says that someone goes in once a week to clean and care for the grounds, but no one seems to know when they go. I've heard stories about the grand parties the family had, and if you go by at the right time, you can almost hear the music, smell the barbecue, and see the lights in the house."

Our ride ended rather abruptly as raindrops began to pelt us, thunder boomed, and lightning flashed. Si and I ran for cover in an old farm shed and waited out the storm. As soon as it ended, we raced to meet my parents for dinner.

Mom and Dad approved of my new friend. We saw Si home, touched base with his dad, and made our way to our temporary lodging. Camping out in a large room upstairs, I fell asleep almost before my head touched the pillow. The next morning sunlight streamed through the enormous window. I stretched and looked around the room, which had definitely belonged to a girl not much older than me.

An elegant mirror hung above a small dressing table along one wall. A study desk and chair set against another. In front of the other window was an ornate window seat where a young lady could watch the night sky or listen to whispers from her "beau" down below.

I got up, put on khaki shorts, a green tee shirt, socks and athletic shoes, and pulled my chestnut hair into a ponytail with a green ribbon to match. I ran downstairs to wash my face and brush my teeth in the only working bathroom and noticed my sparkling green eyes in the reflection.

Mom and Dad were already busy at work at the kitchen table. "Cereal okay, Hon?" Mom asked.

"Sure," I responded, reaching for the cereal and milk. Bringing my bowl to the table, I listened as Mom and Dad discussed the potential real estate value of the house, the turn around, and their profit.

Dad inquired, "Whatcha doin' today, Sadie girl?"

"Maybe I'll see what's on Si's plate," I answered.

Dad nodded his head and Mom smiled a knowing smile. We are a lot alike, so she knew I wouldn't miss a chance to see something new and exciting.

Out the door, I took a quick inventory of the farm. One building resembled an old barn, and a shed looked like a good place for drying tobacco. Farm workers had probably lived in the small gray houses. Their crumbled remains lined the driveway. Then I noticed a window near the chimney on the back of the main house. I put that into my memory bank to check on when I returned.

I rode along the bumpy cobblestone driveway and onto the smoother paved roads into town. As I wheeled up to the drugstore, Si was sweeping off the sidewalk. "Hey, Sadie! What's up?" he called.

"I thought I'd explore a little more today," I answered.

"Come meet my mother first." A beautiful brunette woman with warm brown eyes smiled a friendly smile. "So you're Sadie, the new friend my son praises!"

Mrs. Bartlett was one of the news anchors at the local television station WRAP or "The Rap" as it was called. She said it was good to meet me, kissed her tall blue-eyed red haired husband and their mirror image son goodbye, and left for work.

Si told me, "I have to work until 1:00 today. I'll take you around after that." I agreed to be back by then.

Later, I rode bumpily back up the oak canopied cobblestone driveway and laid my bike on the ground. I climbed the steps to the house and entered to see my mom polishing the brass lamp fixtures. Dad had driven to the city to check on some specialty items. I grabbed a bottle of water from the fridge and called, "I'm going upstairs."

"Okay," I heard my mom respond.

The Treasure

Wondering what lurked upstairs in the attic, I climbed the grand staircase seemingly forever until I reached its door. Proud to have remembered my flashlight, I turned it on and jiggled the doorknob. Nothing happened. I tried again. Still nothing. Finally, I pushed the door. It moved! I shoved once more, and it opened a little. After nudging further, I entered the room. Through the window I'd seen on the back of the house, light poured in. Boots and shoes of long ago lined one whole wall. Trunks and storage boxes stacked high filled another. All kinds of hats with net, veils, ribbons and ties covered a third. I walked to one box, opened it and pulled out a very old but beautiful gown of dark green satin, cream silk and lace. Gold braid encased its tiny covered buttons. Someone certainly had loved the "finer things".

"Sadie," I heard Mom calling all too soon.

"I'm coming," I replied, closed the door reluctantly, and left my treasure.

Lots of Questions

I met Si as planned and, after drinking large glasses of lemonade, we began exploring the town. Turning left from Magnolia Lane, I noticed the homes were much the same as the others we had seen. Some small farms we passed, all of similar size, appeared to be working farms. The wide verandas welcomed visitors with large rocking chairs, small tables, and chairs for tea. Oddly, each home displayed a United States flag in exactly the same way and in the same location.

I looked at Si and inquired cautiously, "Why are the flags like that?"

"Well," he responded, "these homes have been in the same families for years. Their sons fought in the Civil War, World War I and World War II. These homes are full of stories from each era."

"Why don't the Reynolds and McCay houses have flags?" I wondered out loud.

"They would if someone lived there to display them," Si answered.

We resumed our ride in silence. Dusk was coming and we both needed to get home.

"See you tomorrow?" I asked.

"Sure," Si answered. "I'll get off at 5:00. Maybe you could come over and see my Mom's collection."

"What collection?" I asked.

"I'll let it be a surprise," Si teased.

I reached home in record time. Even though Mom loved reconstruction, she also loved to cook. I smelled a delicious, tantalizing aroma coming from the kitchen, where Mom was just taking a chicken pot pie from the oven. After a big helping, a salad, banana pudding and lots of talk about each family member's day, I headed upstairs.

Almost to my bedroom door, I felt a strange pull to return to the attic. I climbed the stairs, opened the door, and switched on the lights. The small lamps cast an eerie glow in the room, and I realized something I had not observed the other day. The attic was divided into sections. The first depicted life in the 1860's. The next smaller one echoed the early 1900's, and the third unmistakably represented the 1940's. Who had organized this and why did they do it? I was tired and decided to look for answers tomorrow.

Breakfast

The next morning at breakfast, I questioned my parents relentlessly.

"Do you know anything about the family who lived here?"

Dad slid back in his chair and gave me a reflective look. "A little," he answered.

"Have you seen the attic?" I demanded.

"Not really," Mom responded. "We were so taken with the rest of the house, we never went to see it."

"Do you know anything about the town?"

Dad chimed in, "It's a true southern town with southern architecture and charm."

"But do you know the people?" I pressed.

I was bursting with questions and yearning for answers!

The Attic

I couldn't meet Si until 5:00, so I had all day to explore. Reaching the top of the stairs to the attic, I slowly pushed the door open. How could I not have seen the careful organization before?

I began going through the beautiful old southern gowns, hats, and shoes. If they could speak, they would tell stories of a very different time—one of love and hate. But, wait, what was this? A small box set upon a stool caught my eye. I opened it gently to find a lovely cameo suspended by a black velvet ribbon. I lifted the delicate object to discover a letter resting underneath and shivered as I removed the paper from the envelope.

It read:

September 1, 1863

My dear cousin Eliza,

I hope this letter finds you well. My life is rather upside down since my husband is away serving with our soldiers. Sometimes I am very scared that I will never see him again, and yet I know I must be strong.

We work hard in the garden each day. It helps us keep our minds occupied. I hope it will not be long until we are all together again.

Please write to me soon.

I remain your loving cousin,

Sadie

"Sadie?" I asked myself. "That's odd," I thought aloud.

Wanting to process this surprising turn of events, I ran downstairs to grab a quick lunch of a PB and J sandwich, an apple, and a glass of milk. Then, as curious as ever, I darted back upstairs to dig further.

Back in the attic, I opened a small wooden box containing some dainty handwork pieces, which had been frequently used. Beneath one of them, I found another letter. I unfolded the brittle paper and read the pencil writing.

October 18, 1918

Dear Macie,

I am sitting here on the cool day in front of the fire. The baby is sleeping now. Ollie and his brother have gone to the quartet convention and Azalee has gone to church. The girl you met when you were here was married last Sunday. Her new husband left on Thursday for the war. I do wish it would come to an end. I must close for now. I certainly enjoyed your visit. I hope you will be able to come again soon.

I remain your devoted sister,

Ressie

(The above is a copy of an original 1918 letter which belongs to the author.)

Staying

"Sadie," Mom called, "can you come here for a minute?"

I was jolted back to the present. I carefully placed the letter back inside the box where it had lived for years.

"Coming, Mom," I replied, closed the door, and bounded down the stairs. When I reached the drawing room, I saw Mom and Dad sitting together on the settee.

"We've been talking," Dad began. When my parents talked, it usually meant trouble for me.

Mom chimed in, "We thought that since we still have an enormous amount of work here that we might need to stay longer than we had expected, at least until Christmas."

I thought for a moment. Transferring schools wouldn't be so bad since I was accustomed to change and "rolling with the punches." Besides, I had already made one friend and I still had many unanswered questions. This house and town had its secrets, and I was determined to uncover them.

I met Si at the drugstore at 5:00 sharp. After finishing up, he put away his broom and white jacket. "See you in a while, Dad," he called. We headed out the door, jumped on our bikes, and pedaled down the street.

I broke the silence. "My parents asked me how I would feel about living here for the rest of the year while they continue working on the house."

"You mean you would go to school here?" Si asked.

"That's right."

"I could show you around and help you get involved at school," Si offered.

We soon arrived at Si's house. Mrs. Bartlett met us at the door. She looked more like a model than anyone's mom.

"What do I smell?" Si asked excitedly.

"Smells like spaghetti to me," Mrs. Bartlett responded as she continued making a huge salad. "Here, have a carrot," she said and tossed one our way. "Other than dinner, what do you two have on your minds?" Mrs. Bartlett inquired.

The Collection

"Well, I thought you might share your collection with Sadie," Si replied.

"My collection?" Mrs. Bartlett asked.

"You know, the pictures and letters."

"Certainly," Mrs. Bartlett headed toward the office and returned with a curious smile. "Sadie, are you a history buff?"

"Well, I almost have to be, since my parents are always reconstructing and refurbishing old houses."

While the sauce bubbled, the three of us poured over letters and pictures of men from the Civil War to World War I and World War II.

"Here's a letter dated April 15,1863," I observed, "and another from October, 1918, and one dated December 7, 1941. You know, I found some old clothes, letters, books, and trunks in the attic of the McCay house. I wonder what else is lurking up there?"

Mrs. Bartlett was intrigued and chatted excitedly about the treasures they had shared. "I've been working on a human interest story about our town and its unsung heroes. If you find anything interesting, please let me know."

Following a delicious dinner, I thanked the Bartlett's and excused myself to pedal home. Si rode beside me on his bike.

The next day, Saturday, I awoke to large raindrops hitting my window panes. No outdoor explorations today. Since Si had to work anyway, it looked like the perfect time for digging through the trunks and clothes upstairs. I dressed quickly and once more climbed the steps to the attic. I turned on the lights and examined dress after dress. The attic was a regular costume shop, except these garments were originals.

Slowly, I began to open boxes. In the first, I found several newspaper clippings. One dated December 7, 1941, described the attack on Pearl Harbor. A different one encouraged people on the home front to collect aluminum to be made into airplanes. More fascinated than ever, I picked up one article after another. The age of the newspaper archive provided each clipping with a yellow border, but the information was anything but yellow. It was as red, white, and blue as it could be.

News story after news story told of battles, the wounded, and those who gave their lives for our country and its freedom. One letter buried in the bottom of the box caught my attention. Its envelope was addressed with firm, neat handwriting to "Sadie McCay." I gasped, nervously opened it and began to read:

Dear Sadie,

I just wanted you to know that I am safe for now. I think of you often, and I cannot wait to get home. Maybe things will be better soon.

Love,
Silas Bartlett

Thoughtfully, I slipped the letter back into its envelope.No wonder my parents were so taken with this old house! Their decisions now made complete sense. After all, what was my mom's maiden name? Why, it was McCay!

"Wait until I tell Si what I found!"

Sadie McCay

After more reading, I pieced together information about Sadie McCay and Silas Bartlett:

Sadie, born in 1920, was the only daughter of the town's sole doctor. Growing up, she laughed, played, and worked helping her father in his office as often as she could. When World War II began, she left for a military hospital stateside in Savannah. Her high school beau, Si, exercised his patriotic duty by enlisting in the military, and left for the fighting. Sadie worked day in and day out, trying to forget how worried she was about Si by helping her patients. Sometimes she offered to stay late so that others could go home to their children.

Silas Bartlett

The oldest son of his druggist father and school teacher mother, Silas Bartlett felt a deep love for God, family, and country. Thus, when the military called for volunteers, he gave up his family, his girlfriend, and his education to enlist. The importance of freedom was always uppermost in his mind. "When this war ends," he thought, "I'll go back home to Sadie, my folks, and my education." As it turned out, that is exactly what he did.

I snapped out of my reverie in the attic. Even though the sun was still hidden, the rain had stopped. I descended the stairs to the second floor and then to the first, thinking of my newfound discoveries about my ancestry. I walked into the kitchen as if in a daze and saw Dad sitting at the table.

"Well, where have you been all day?" Dad asked.

I smiled slowly and answered, "Finding out who I am."

Dad raised his eyebrows with an inquisitive look. "Tell me more."

My eyes widened. "I learned that Mom's family has owned this house since before the Civil War. I also found that my great grandmother was Silas Bartlett's "girl" and became his wife."

"It all makes sense to me now why you and Mom wanted to come here. But, why didn't you tell me?" I inquired.

My mom walked into the kitchen and asked, "What's going on?"

Dad responded quickly, "It seems our detective daughter has discovered our secret."

Mom smiled, "Well, just what have you found out?"

I began to share my findings. I still couldn't believe the connections between the McCays and the Bartletts.

Remembering my exploits with Si, I questioningly looked at my dad. "I don't suppose you know anything about the Reynolds house, do you?"

"Guilty on that part, too," he responded. "My grandparents and parents looked after the place as long as possible. Working away from here, I paid caretakers monthly to keep the homestead going and to be quiet about who hired them."

I swiped my forehead. "This is a lot for me to take in. Wait until I tell Si!"

Meanwhile, Mrs. Barlett, doing research at the local library, discovered the story behind the homes on Valor Street.

Sandra Thurman

Valor Street

When the cotton mill came to town, the company built houses for its employees. Later the huge foundry arrived and followed suit. The houses, all built alike, eventually took on the individual personalities of the families who inhabited each one.

Most of the families' boys joined the military when each of the World Wars came along. Some of the girls went to work in the factories to replace the men. Others helped the Red Cross or collected aluminum and rubber, important war materials in short supply.

A blue patriotic star was hung in a home's window to stand for each child in military service. The saddest times were when a heartbroken family changed a blue star to a somber gold color to show that their child had died for his country. One family was very proud to have four sons in service and grieved when each one gave his life so that America could remain free. Yet, even in such difficult times, PATRIOTISM reigned.

The Celebration

The next week, as my parents and I made our way to town to attend a celebration, a carnival-like atmosphere pervaded. After driving through crowded roads and passing blocked streets, we parked as close to Main Street as possible and walked towards the event. Smells of popcorn and peanuts wafted through the air. Motorcycle engines reverberated. In the distance, the local high school band marched our way playing instruments. Red, white, and blue floats lined up one after the other for a parade.

Mrs. Bartlett, the award-winning news anchor and town historian, spoke into her mic before television cameras. "Good afternoon. This is Whitney Bartlett from WRAP-TV. We are here for a wonderful celebration of heroes! The color guard from the local high school is just ahead of the mayor and the master of ceremonies. Behind the mayor's car are floats of various shapes and sizes. Each one illustrates pride in our country."

Strains of patriotic music filled the air. The Patriot Guard escorted a horse-drawn caisson to honor those who had given their all for their country, reminding us that "freedom isn't free."

After the parade, the mayor and other officials gave speeches. The most exciting occurrence was hearing the whir of a helicopter, seeing it land in a cleared space, and witnessing the governor of our state emerge. On the lawn of City Hall, he presented the mayor with a plaque stating that the sacrifice and service of the town had earned it the title of "The Most Patriotic Small Town in America."

My new friend Si and I stood smack dab in the middle of all the celebration. Watching with eager eyes, we realized that our ancestors, though not the well known stars of history, were definitely important characters in the plot of American Patriotism. The heroes who had preceded us in a simple small community were examples for us to follow in the small town of Sacrifice!

"I'm beginning to understand why we place significance on celebrating July 4th, Veteran's Day, and Memorial Day," I thought to myself. "These days are reminders of others' sacrifice for us and our country."

Waking me from my thoughts, I heard a familiar voice, "This is Whitney Bartlett from WRAP-TV, signing off in Sacrifice, a small town of patriotism and hope."

Printed in the United States
By Bookmasters